ADAPTING TO CLIMATE CHANGE

BY EMMA HUDDLESTON

CONTENT CONSULTANT
Atreyee Bhattacharya, PhD
Research Affiliate, Institute of Arctic and Alpine Research
University of Colorado Boulder;
Visiting Researcher, Scripps Institution of Oceanography
University of California San Diego

Cover image: Growing plants on the sides of buildings can help buildings stay cool.

Core Library

An Imprint of Abdo Publishing
abdobooks.com

abdobooks.com

Published by Abdo Publishing, a division of ABDO, PO Box 398166, Minneapolis, Minnesota 55439.
Copyright © 2021 by Abdo Consulting Group, Inc. International copyrights reserved in all countries.
No part of this book may be reproduced in any form without written permission from the publisher.
Core Library™ is a trademark and logo of Abdo Publishing.

Printed in the United States of America, North Mankato, Minnesota
082020
012021

THIS BOOK CONTAINS
RECYCLED MATERIALS

Cover Photo: Oskar Hellebaut/Shutterstock Images
Interior Photos: iStockphoto, 4–5, 19, 20, 32, 45; Rick Rycroft/AP Images, 8–9; Shutterstock Images,
10, 14–15, 31, 43; Red Line Editorial, 12; O. Vasik/iStockphoto, 18; Andrea Leiber/Shutterstock
Images, 22; Mark Wilson/Getty Images News/Getty Images, 24–25; Steve Geer/iStockphoto, 27;
Indranil Mukherjee/AFP/Getty Images, 28; Richard Baker/In Pictures/Getty Images, 34–35; Golden
Sikorka/Shutterstock Images, 37; Gerald Herbert/AP Images, 40

Editor: Marie Pearson
Series Designer: Katharine Hale

Library of Congress Control Number: 2019954178

Publisher's Cataloging-in-Publication Data

Names: Huddleston, Emma, author
Title: Adapting to climate change / by Emma Huddleston
Description: Minneapolis, Minnesota : Abdo Publishing, 2021 | Series: Climate change | Includes
    online resources and index.
Identifiers: ISBN 9781532192715 (lib. bdg.) | ISBN 9781644944240 (pbk.) | ISBN 9781098210618
    (ebook)
Subjects: LCSH: Climatic changes--Juvenile literature. | Adaptation to heat--Juvenile literature. |
    Adaptation (Biology)--Juvenile literature. | Atmospheric greenhouse effect--Juvenile literature.
Classification: DDC 363.738--dc23

CONTENTS

SHRINKING HABITAT

A field of white flowers shakes gently in the wind. Sunshine brightens the sky. Black-and-yellow bumblebees buzz from flower to flower. They sip sweet, sticky nectar from the flowers. Then they take some back to their hive. There, other bumblebees turn the nectar into honey. Honey is food for bees during winter months when flowers are not in bloom.

The bees' lifestyle has been the same for a very long time. What has changed is where

Bumblebees are losing their homes due to climate change.

they are living. Bumblebees are moving to higher elevations with cooler temperatures. Their southern habitats are too warm. Relocating is one way to adapt. Adapting is changing in order to survive. The southern part of the bumblebees' range is moving north. But the northern part of their habitat isn't shifting. So overall, bumblebees are losing space. Their habitat is shrinking. In order to survive, they may have to adapt another way. However, adapting is not easy. Most plants and animals struggle to deal with warming temperatures.

WHAT IS CLIMATE CHANGE?

Climate change is shifts in Earth's weather patterns over time. Changes in the atmosphere start these shifts. One of the effects of climate change is rising temperatures. Rising temperatures lead to sea level rise, ice melt, and extreme weather. All of these effects can make life more difficult for plants, animals, and people. Stronger storms can damage cities. Melting land ice adds to rising sea levels. Rising sea levels can wash away coastlines where people and animals live. Climate change also makes other natural threats such as fires and droughts worse.

Climate change is happening because there are more greenhouse gases in the air than there were in the past. Greenhouse gases include carbon dioxide, methane, and nitrous oxide. The term *greenhouse gas* comes from how the gases trap heat in Earth's atmosphere. They work in a similar way to how a glass greenhouse traps the sun's heat.

PERSPECTIVES

CLIMATE CHANGE IS A THREAT

Katharine Hayhoe was one of the authors of the 2019 US climate assessment. The report gathers data about climates across the United States. Authors of the 2019 edition found that climate change puts both people and nature at risk of more severe weather. When asked about the most serious consequence of climate change, Hayhoe said, "If I could pick a single way to explain climate change to everyone it would be threat multiplier." Threat multiplier refers to how climate change causes dangerous events such as storms to become more frequent. The report encouraged people to adapt in ways such as building stronger homes in coastal areas.

Scientists believe climate change played a role in the dry conditions that led to major wildfires in Australia from 2019 to 2020.

Earth needs greenhouse gases to stay warm. But too much of them causes Earth's temperature to rise. Earth's average temperature in 2019 was nearly 1.8 degrees Fahrenheit (1°C) warmer than the temperature in 1969. The warming is happening at a faster rate than life on Earth can adapt.

Human activity has increased greenhouse gases in the atmosphere for more than 100 years. Burning

fossil fuels such as oil and coal releases greenhouse gases. Today, climate change wouldn't end immediately even if people stopped emitting all greenhouse gases. But people can make the future effects less severe by reducing carbon emissions. They also can adapt to the current effects of climate change. They can find ways to live with the effects.

One way people adapt is by improving how crops grow in challenging conditions. In 2014 scientists

Industrial growth has resulted in an increase of carbon dioxide and other greenhouse gases that trap heat.

created a soybean that could grow using less water than other soybeans. Climate change is causing droughts to become more common in some areas. A soybean that grows using less water is important for dry regions. Other soybeans might not survive in these areas.

FOCUSING ON SOLUTIONS

People can't rely on adaptation alone. Most plants and animals aren't able to adapt quickly enough. The warming is happening too rapidly. Resources people rely on, such as wood and water, will disappear. People must use mitigation along with adaptation. Mitigation means reducing the amount of greenhouse gases put into the air. The goal is to slow climate change enough that life can adapt. Using renewable energy is an example of mitigation. Renewable energy is

ADAPTATION PROJECTS

People can adapt to climate change in many ways. Some projects happen before a disaster strikes. Other projects happen in response to an event or problem. Projects can be a series of small steps over time. Cleaning up a beach and maintaining it happens bit by bit. On the other hand, some projects involve one big change. For example, a person might leave a beachfront home and move to a new area. Adaptation projects can be done by one person or a large group. All types of adaptation are important for addressing climate change.

SOURCES OF US GREENHOUSE GAS EMISSIONS, 2018

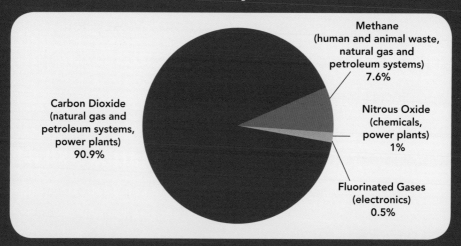

Methane (human and animal waste, natural gas and petroleum systems) 7.6%

Nitrous Oxide (chemicals, power plants) 1%

Carbon Dioxide (natural gas and petroleum systems, power plants) 90.9%

Fluorinated Gases (electronics) 0.5%

This chart shows what percentage each type of greenhouse gas contributed to total US emissions in 2018. It also explains some of the main sources of each type of gas. Many human activities put greenhouse gases into the air. How can knowing where the gases come from help people adapt?

power that comes from natural sources that won't run out. These sources include sunlight, wind, or water movement. Using renewable energy lowers greenhouse gas emissions.

Climate change has effects that can be tackled in many different ways. People must work together to fix the problems it causes. They must work to help the planet adapt to the effects for decades to come.

STRAIGHT TO THE
SOURCE

The Global Commission on Adaptation encourages people to adapt to climate change. Its 2019 report explained why it is important to both adapt to and mitigate climate change:

> *To a certain point, incremental approaches will suffice, such as continued improvements in water management or conventional approaches for flood protection and land use. But that may not always be the case. . . . For example, protecting against or accommodating sea-level rise in low-lying areas may no longer be possible—and coastal residents may need to . . . retreat. . . .*
>
> *Even with the most ambitious adaptation actions, we will face residual climate impacts. For this reason, ambitious mitigation is the best form of adaptation. . . . Choosing between adaptation and mitigation is a false choice—we must do both.*

Source: "Adapt Now." *Global Commission on Adaptation*, 13 Sept. 2019, cdn.gca.org, p.10. Accessed 3 Feb. 2020.

WHAT'S THE BIG IDEA?

The authors of this report are using evidence to support a point. Write a paragraph describing the point the authors are making. Then write down two or three pieces of evidence the authors use to make the point.

PLANTS AND ANIMALS ADAPT

Plant and animal species can respond to climate change in three ways. One response is moving to new locations. To deal with rising temperatures, hundreds of species are moving to higher ground or closer to the poles. They are searching for cooler climates. Trees in the Amazon rain forest in South America are growing on higher ground to survive. As new seeds scatter, those that land on higher ground grow better than ones that land in lower habitats.

The Amazon rain forest contains 10 percent of the world's known species. Many will be threatened by climate change if they can't adapt.

TREES AND CLIMATE CHANGE

Planting trees is one way to help mitigate climate change. Like other plants, trees take in carbon dioxide, sunlight, and water to make food. This process is called photosynthesis. Some extra carbon dioxide that trees don't use gets stored in their trunk and leaves. Storing carbon dioxide in plants keeps it out of the air. For this reason, planting trees is a natural and cheap solution to climate change. However, people must be careful about where and how many trees are added to an area. Trees need the right conditions to grow. If the trees die, they release carbon dioxide back into the air.

A second response to climate change is to evolve. Species evolve slowly over time. They pass on to the next generation certain traits that help them survive. Eventually unhelpful traits no longer exist. But climate change is happening quickly. Most species can't keep up. A species can adapt to a change of 1.8 degrees Fahrenheit (1°C) over 1 million years. Earth is warming much faster than that.

The warming temperatures are disrupting natural cycles, such as when birds nest or when animals migrate. In some cases, climate change causes plants to flower and insects to emerge too soon. For example, flowers may bloom before pollinators are active. Pollinators are animals that spread pollen. Pollen is necessary to help flowers make seeds.

RESTORING FORESTS

Scientist Tom Crowther believes planting trees and creating healthy forests is a valuable response to climate change. He said in 2019, "Our study shows clearly that forest restoration is the best climate change solution available today. . . . If we act now, this could cut carbon dioxide in the atmosphere by up to 25 percent, to levels last seen almost a century ago."

In forests, soil also stores large amounts of carbon dioxide. Sometimes soil stores twice as much as trees. But warmer temperatures and sunlight exposure can make soil break down faster. When soil breaks down, it lets carbon dioxide back into the air.

Low water levels caused by drought can make it difficult for some salmon to reach their breeding grounds.

The third response is a plastic change. The word *plastic* refers to a change in a living thing in response to the environment, not the material plastic. The change is not genetic. Instead, it is a change in something such as behavior or speed of development. Temperature or other environmental factors can cause the change. Some Pacific salmon can raise their heart rates in warm waters. Swimming in warm water takes more energy for the salmon. A faster-beating heart means more blood flow, which helps the salmon stay alive. Blood carries nutrients and energy throughout its body.

PLANT LIFE

Some plants are adapting to climate change. Wild thyme can make strong-smelling oil to protect itself. Animals avoid eating the thyme when it smells. But being covered in oil is a risk. Oily thyme can freeze and die in cold temperatures. In recent years, wild thyme has been making more oil. It is taking a risk to survive. It is making more oil because cold temperatures have been less common in recent years. The plant is less

As temperatures warm, wild thyme is able to produce more oil to protect itself from being eaten.

likely to freeze. So now it can protect itself even better against being eaten.

Some cold places such as Russia, Canada, and China are gaining growing days. Growing days are days when the temperature is right for plants to grow. It is not too hot or too cold. But hot, tropical regions may lose growing days. More days will become too hot to grow. Additionally a lack of water and changes in the soil could limit the amount of nutrients available for plants to grow.

CHANGING TEMPERATURES AND COLORS

Wildlife adapts to climate change in many ways. Some adaptations are easy for scientists to see. Tawny owls have brown or gray feathers. In some northern European countries, the gray tawny owl was more common. Its feathers blend in better with the snow. But because of warmer temperatures, tawny owls' habitats

Brown tawny owls are becoming more common than gray ones because of climate change.

Banded snails with light-colored shells can handle heat better than snails with darker shells.

now have less snow. The brown owls are becoming more common. Their feathers blend in with brown tree bark and soil.

Similarly, banded snails are changing colors because of climate change. The snail's shell color is genetic. It is determined by genes passed down from parents. The gene that controls shell color is also affected by body temperature. Snails with light-colored shells have a cooler body temperature. This helps them survive in warm places. Snails with darker shells have a higher body temperature. These snails live in shady places. Higher body temperatures keep snails warm in places with little sunlight. However, scientists have noticed more and more banded snails with light-colored shells. Even snails that live in shady places aren't often getting genes for dark-colored shells. They are being passed genes to help them adapt and stay cool in rising temperatures.

FURTHER EVIDENCE

Chapter Two talks about plants and animals adapting to survive. Identify the main point and some key supporting evidence. Then look at the website below. Find a quote that supports the chapter's main point. Does the quote support a piece of evidence already in the chapter? Or does it add a new piece of information?

WHAT IS CLIMATE CHANGE?

abdocorelibrary.com/adapting-to-climate-change

CHANGES TO LAND AND WATER

Climate change is making natural threats such as storms worse. Governments must find new ways to protect people. This is especially important for coastal cities. These cities are at greater risk of flooding. Hurricanes bring heavy rainfall. Because cities have a lot of pavement, there is little open ground to soak up the water. Porous pavement can help make flooding less of a risk. Porous pavement has spaces that allow water to soak through.

Hurricane Dorian caused floods of up to 7 feet (2 m) in North Carolina in 2019.

The water can then reach the ground. The flooding is less severe.

Riverbank armor can strengthen the banks of rivers. The armor can be made of plants that have deep roots. It can be added to the edges of rivers or lakes to hold back loose soil or rocks. This keeps the banks from washing away, which can lead to flooding. Retaining walls can also hold back riverbanks.

NATURAL STORM PROTECTION

Plants also are useful in protecting against extreme weather. They can soak up extra water from floods. Their leaves and roots can block waves from crashing farther inland. The natural state of riverbanks protects areas on the edge of water. A soft armor of plant life on the shore shields against waves and rising water. Medium-sized ragged rocks or pieces of concrete called riprap act as riverbank armor. Sometimes people add things to a natural riverbank. People build up its defenses by adding more plants or rocks.

Rocks have been placed along the shore of Lake Michigan to help protect the shoreline.

This strengthens the riverbank. In Iowa City, Iowa, the local government grew more plants near the Iowa River to protect against floods.

Coastal mangroves are another natural storm protection. A mangrove is a group of trees and shrubs with tangled roots above ground. Mangroves grow in places with changing water levels. They act as a

buffer against floods and strong waves. People have destroyed mangroves or drained the land around them to build cities. In order to protect coastlines from the stronger storms caused by climate change, mangroves need to be restored.

Dry areas also benefit from plants. These areas are at risk of droughts or wildfires. But certain grasses, shrubs, and trees with deep roots can protect

Some people in India work to restore coastal mangroves.

the area. These plants block wind and create shade for the soil. Shade helps the soil stay wet and cool. Blocking wind lowers the risk of quickly spreading wildfires.

SMART FARMING

Smart farming methods can help people adapt to climate change. In areas where water is becoming scarce, farmers can work to not waste water. Technology can help them water their fields responsibly. It can measure how wet or dry the soil is. Weather radar can tell how much rain is likely in the area. Then farmers can know how much additional water their fields need.

Farmers also can plant cover crops in

FLOATING FARMS

In Bangladesh, 75 percent of the country can flood in certain years. Farmers can't use traditional land farming methods or the crops would drown. Instead, many farmers use floating farms. The farms are made of strips of land that rise and fall with water levels during rainy seasons.

In areas that experience drought, it is important that farmers water only when necessary.

Crimson clover can be used as a cover crop. Cover crops help protect and enrich the soil. They also attract pollinators.

rotation with main crops. Some farmers grow radishes or clover between seasons of growing corn, soy, or cotton. The leaves and roots of radishes and clover protect the fields from severe weather. The leaves block the wind. They keep the soil from drying out. Leaves also shield soil from heavy rains. The roots hold the soil together and keep it from washing away.

STRAIGHT TO THE
SOURCE

David Wolfe is a professor at Cornell University in New York. He studies how climate change affects crop growth. He said:

> *I never expected . . . that one of the most important things that would come up with regards to the fruit crop growers is actually cold and frost damage in a warming world. The reason for that is that these plants can sometimes be tricked into blooming earlier with a warming winter. . . .*
>
> *Farmers may have to consider misting systems or wind machines for frost protection. And our apple breeders may have to think about coming up with genetic types that don't jump the gun in terms of early bloom in warm winters."*

Source: Cornell Climate Smart Farming. "Climate Smart Farming Story." *YouTube*, 29 Sept. 2015, youtube.com. Accessed 21 Jan. 2020.

CONSIDER YOUR AUDIENCE

Review this passage closely. Consider how you would adapt it for a different audience, such as your younger friends. Write a blog post so that it can be understood by them. How does your new approach differ from the original text, and why?

BUILDINGS AND COMMUNITIES

Climate change affects the whole world. People can make changes to buildings to stay safe. Houses are made out of wood. Wood catches fire easily. In areas where wildfires are becoming more common, houses easily burn down. Builders can add metal coverings over wood to make it more fire resistant. This can make it harder for homes to burn.

As the climate warms, people use more energy to keep buildings cool. If the energy

Many cities do not have much land area for plants, so architects have designed rooftop gardens.

BREATHING BAD AIR

Air pollutants include carbon dioxide, smoke, mold, pollen, methane, and soot. High amounts of these gases and particles can be harmful when breathed in. Breathing polluted air over many years can lead to health issues. People have higher risks of disease, asthma, stroke, and cancer. The World Health Organization estimates that each year 3.8 million people die earlier than they would otherwise because of air pollution. Of those people, 80 percent die from heart disease or stroke. The other 20 percent die from respiratory illness or cancer.

comes from fossil fuels, that only adds to climate change. One way people can adapt buildings to the warming temperatures is by adding plants. Green roofs are layers of soil and plants on top of buildings. The plants take in sunlight to grow. They keep layers below them, such as the soil and roof, cool. Normal roofing materials absorb heat. They make the building warmer. Green roofs keep buildings cooler without using energy. This lets people use less energy to keep

LAYERS OF A
GREEN ROOF

A green roof is a building adaptation to help deal with climate change. How is a green roof a man-made solution? How is it a natural solution?

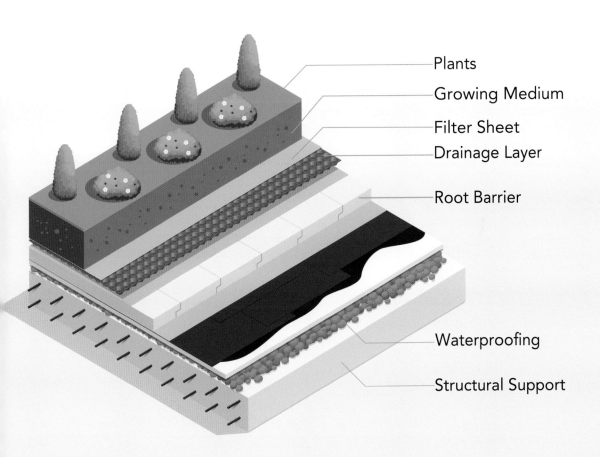

Plants

Growing Medium

Filter Sheet

Drainage Layer

Root Barrier

Waterproofing

Structural Support

their homes and businesses cool. Additionally, green roofs absorb water from rainfall. They can help cities deal with extra rainfall caused by climate change.

Another benefit of using green roofs is they help mitigate climate change. The plants take in carbon from the air. This lowers the greenhouse gases in the atmosphere.

REDESIGNING CITIES

When a storm hits, power lines are prone to damage. Fallen power lines can cut off electricity from homes and businesses.

They also can be dangerous. People can get electrocuted. Cities can bury power lines to protect them from extreme weather.

Sometimes, the only answer is to move away from a problem. Major floods hit Tulsa, Oklahoma, in 1974 and 1984. The waters destroyed buildings. People wanted to make changes to prepare for more disasters that might happen. They spoke to city leaders and asked them to help. Over time, the city raised money. Leaders moved more than 1,000 buildings away from water. Then they banned building in areas prone to flooding to keep people safe.

GLOBAL CHANGES

Adapting to climate change is important. Even if people stopped emissions now, the world would still feel the effects of climate change for centuries. Some adaptation is happening now. Other people are planning for the future. Coastal cities are at risk of flooding. They face an increased risk of extreme weather such as hurricanes.

There are many ways students can help the world adapt to climate change, including restoring wetlands.

To adapt, engineers and scientists have been working on models of floating cities. They would be anchored to land. But they would float on the sea near the coast. The buildings and roads could move up and down with waves. All parts would be made of strong materials that could survive storms.

Adapting to climate change is important. But it is also important to work on slowing and eventually stopping climate change. Many activists have a goal of net-zero emissions. Net-zero means the amount of emissions going into the air equals the amount of emissions taken out of the air by trees and other natural cycles. Achieving this goal would help make future climate change effects less severe.

People may not know exactly what changes and problems will happen in the future. But they can adapt to climate change in many ways to protect people and wildlife. And they can work to reduce its effects by lowering emissions and caring for the world around them.

EXPLORE ONLINE

Chapter Four talks about how communities can adapt to climate change. Visit the website below about rising temperatures in cities. Compare and contrast the information there with information from this chapter. Does the article answer any questions you had about adapting to climate change?

WHAT IS AN URBAN HEAT ISLAND?

abdocorelibrary.com/adapting-to-climate-change

FAST FACTS

- Climate change is a shift in Earth's long-term weather patterns. It leads to global warming, rising sea levels, and extreme weather. These are harming people and wildlife.

- Climate change is caused by rising levels of greenhouse gases in the air. Greenhouse gases include carbon dioxide, methane, and nitrous oxide. They trap and store heat in Earth's atmosphere.

- Adaptation is finding ways to lessen the effects of climate change on daily life. Mitigation is action that helps slow climate change.

- Individuals and governments must work together to adapt to the problems caused by climate change.

- Plants and animals must adapt to survive. They adapt in three main ways. They move to a better habitat. They evolve over time. Or they make a plastic change. But climate change is happening too quickly for most living things to evolve.

- Climate change makes natural threats such as storms worse. People can adapt by using human-made or natural storm protection. Plants or riprap make riverbank armor.

- Natural land features, such as coastal mangroves, help protect nearby cities from flooding.

- Smart farming methods, such as cover crops, can keep soil healthy.

- Green roofs help keep buildings cool while using less energy. They also soak up some of the excess rainfall caused by climate change.

- Global changes are needed to slow down the future effects of carbon emissions.

STOP AND
THINK

Surprise Me

Chapter Two discusses how animals and plants adapt to climate change. After reading this book, what two or three facts about adapting did you find most surprising? Write a few sentences about each fact. Why did you find each fact surprising?

Dig Deeper

After reading this book, what questions do you still have about adapting to climate change? With an adult's help, find a few reliable sources that can help you answer your questions. Write a paragraph about what you learned.

Say What?

Studying science and climate change can mean learning a lot of new vocabulary. Find five words in this book you've never heard before. Use a dictionary to find out what they mean. Then write the meanings in your own words, and use each word in a new sentence.

Take a Stand

Adapting to the effects of climate change is important to keep people safe. But mitigation, or reducing greenhouse gas emissions so that future effects aren't as severe, is also important. Do you think one of these approaches is more valuable than the other? Or are both equally important? Why?

GLOSSARY

archaeologist
a person who studies evidence of past human life

civilization
a group of people living in the same region and time period

emerge
to come out of something

emitting
giving off or sending out

evolve
to change as a species by passing down certain traits over time

gene
a trait passed from parent to offspring, which determines certain behaviors and looks

pollutant
a particle that makes the air, land, or water unhealthy

porous
having holes or openings in the surface

radar
a device that sends out radio waves to locate objects

respiratory
having to do with the lungs, mouth, throat, and the process of breathing

ONLINE RESOURCES

To learn more about adapting to climate change, visit our free resource websites below.

Visit **abdocorelibrary.com** or scan this QR code for free Common Core resources for teachers and students, including vetted activities, multimedia, and booklinks, for deeper subject comprehension.

Visit **abdobooklinks.com** or scan this QR code for free additional online weblinks for further learning. These links are routinely monitored and updated to provide the most current information available.

LEARN MORE

Harris, Duchess. *Environmental Protests.* Abdo Publishing, 2018.

Herman, Gail. *What Is Climate Change?* Penguin Random House, 2018.

London, Martha. *Climate Change and Politics.* Abdo Publishing, 2021.

INDEX

About the Author

Emma Huddleston lives in the Twin Cities with her husband. She enjoys writing children's books about nature and animals. She thinks adapting to climate change is fascinating and important.